FLY

Nathan Clement

BOYDS MILLS PRESS

AN IMPRINT OF HIGHLIGHTS

Honesdale, Pennsylvania

I want to thank . . .
My technical advisors:
First Officer Matthew Conrad
Tim Tallar, aircraft manufacturing
Aram Basmadjian, Chief Flight Instructor at Lehigh Carbon Community
College, Schnecksville, Pennsylvania, for his careful review of the text
and illustrations.
The cast: Sohee, Tara, and Mark VanderWoude;
Donna Stambaugh; and Greta Clement

For information about permission to reproduce selections from this book,
please contact permissions@highlights.com.

Boyds Mills Press
An Imprint of Highlights
815 Church Street
Honesdale, Pennsylvania 18431
boydsmillspress.com
Printed in China

ISBN: 978-1-62979-937-7
Library of Congress Control Number: 2018942685

First edition
10 9 8 7 6 5 4 3 2 1

The text is set in Calibri.
The illustrations are digital.

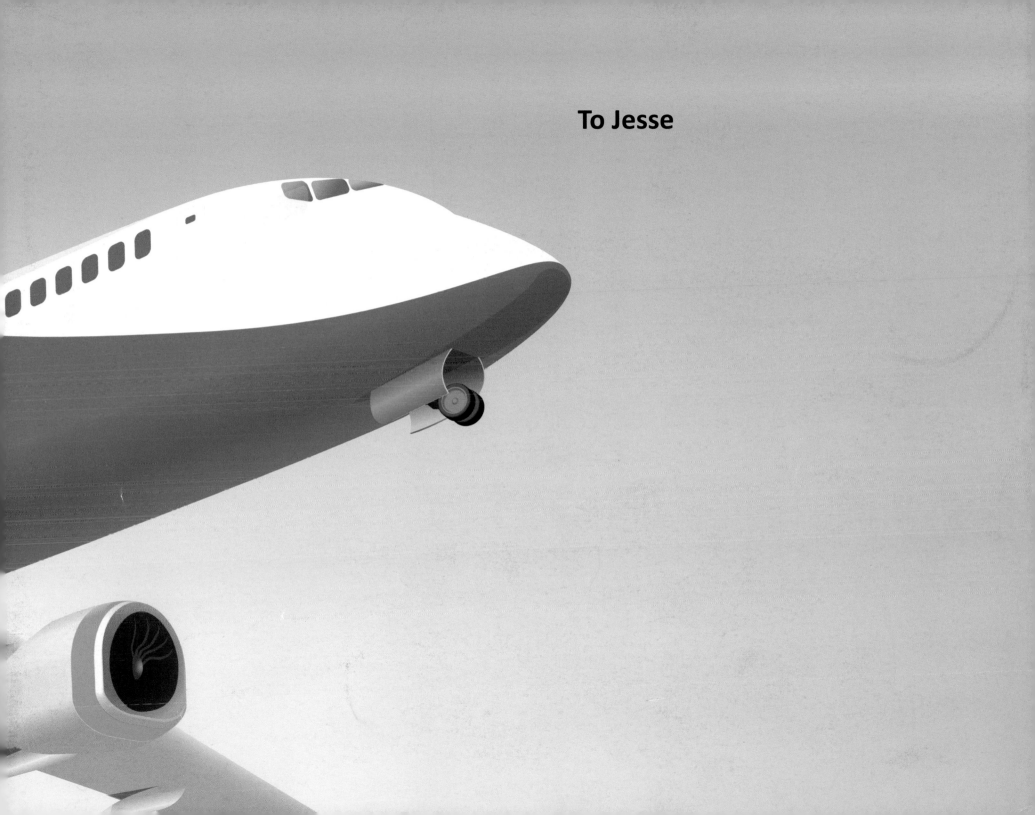

To Jesse

The airport is filled with passengers ready to fly. The gate agent says, "Now boarding!" Passengers present their tickets at the gate.

The baggage crew loads the cargo hold.
"Cargo doors are closed," calls the ground crew.

The pilot calls, "Roger.
Brakes released. Ready for push."

"Roger," says the ground crew.
Then the tug pushes the plane away from the gate.

Ground control in the tower calls, "You are clear to taxi."

Soon the plane rushes down the runway.
The pilot pulls back on the yoke, and the plane
climbs into the air.

Some passengers read. Some watch clouds.
Some snooze.

"Are we flying a long way?" asks a girl.

"Yes," says her mother.
"But it will go fast."

The time flies. Then the pilot announces, "Thank you for flying with us." The flight attendants collect trash, put food service carts back into the galley, and are seated as the plane approaches the airport.

The pilot checks with tower control.
"You're clear to land," they tell her.

"Prepare for landing," the pilot says.
She adjusts the flaps and lowers the landing gear.

The copilot takes the controls
and touches down.

"Smooth," says the pilot.

"Welcome to Indianapolis!" announces the lead flight attendant. "Claim your baggage on carousel six."

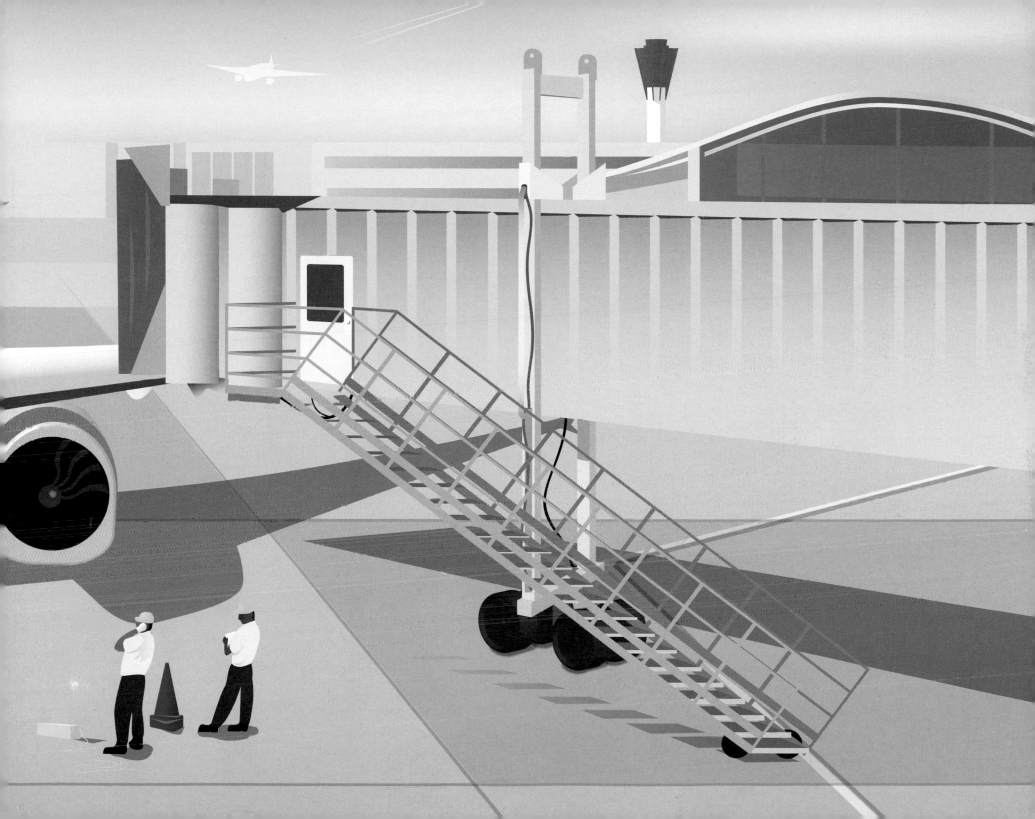

The flight is now over. "Your first flight. You've earned your wings!" says the pilot.

Airplane Words to Know

cargo hold—a space under an airplane for carrying luggage

cockpit—where the pilot sits to fly the plane

flaps—edges on airplane wings that drop down to help the plane slow and land

ground control—help the airplanes on the ground taxi safely

ground crew or **baggage crew**—load an airplane with luggage and push it away from the gate

landing gear—the wheels under an airplane when it's on the ground

roger—"I understand that"

taxi—to "drive" an airplane on the ground

tug or **pushback tractor**—pushes a plane backward on the ground

tower control or **air traffic control**—help the pilot fly in a safe direction

yoke—like a steering wheel, but it makes the airplane go up or down in the air

flight attendant—makes sure everyone flying has what they need and shows them how to be safe

carousel—the machine in an airport that catches the luggage when it comes off the airplane